A Slice of Teenage Life

(not just another teen story)

A Kids' Own Publishing Partnership Book

A Slice of Teenage Life is a collaboration between Kids' Own Publishing Partnership and The National Youth Federation. This project was established after a number of youth workers expressed an interest in making a book with the young people that they work with. The aim of this project is to involve young people in the process of publishing a book from initial ideas to a finished product through a series of masterclasses. We developed teamwork and collaborative ways of working. Four groups participated in the project: Monaghan Youth Service, Midlands Regional Youth Service, Athy Youth Service and Newbridge Youth Service. The groups came together in a series of workshops, which took place over a year. The themes highlighted in this book are Drugs, Friendship, Relationships, Separation and Loss. These raised a number of interesting issues for the participants, which are reflected in their stories. This book is by teenagers, for teenagers. There are four stories in this book: Time Out; Almost Crying; Up, Up and Down; Inside Out. All the stories have been written, illustrated and designed by the teenagers in the project who were between twelve and eighteen years of age.

Orla Kenny Kids' Own Publishing Partnership

The National Youth Federation (NYF) is the largest youth work organisation in the Republic of Ireland. Founded in 1962, the NYF caters for the changing needs of young people by developing and adapting a wide variety of relevant and accessible services. These services are provided at community level through a national network of 20 Local Youth Services. The mission of the National Youth Federation is:
"To actively empower the contribution of all young people in society through their critical participation in local youth services."
The National Youth Federation are delighted to have been involved in such an empowering project where young people wrote about young people's issues and experiences for other young people. It has been a fantastic opportunity for all those involved, both workers and young people, to engage in a dynamic and encompassing programme including research, creative writing, illustration, and design. We would like to take this opportunity to thank all the staff at Kids' Own Publishing Partnership and the youth workers involved and congratulate the young people on their work!

Catherine Kaye, Arts and Programmes Development Officer,
National Youth Federation(NYF).

Time
Out

Hi Ma, I just had an argument with Dad, I hate it without you. You are gone a year now. He doesn't have a clue about taking care of me!

He makes me be in by eight o'clock and that was the time I had to be in at when I was 7 years old. He thinks I'm immature. My Dad is too over protective. I think he's just being selfish. Bye Mum, I'll come back as soon as I can, I miss you.

That's still early, but okay then!

That's dad,
he says to be
in by ten;
he never
leaves me
alone.

Your dad is weird.
Forget about it,
let's go down town.

Watch out for that car!

aahh!

She is my
best mate

I'm so sorry. I'll call an ambulance.

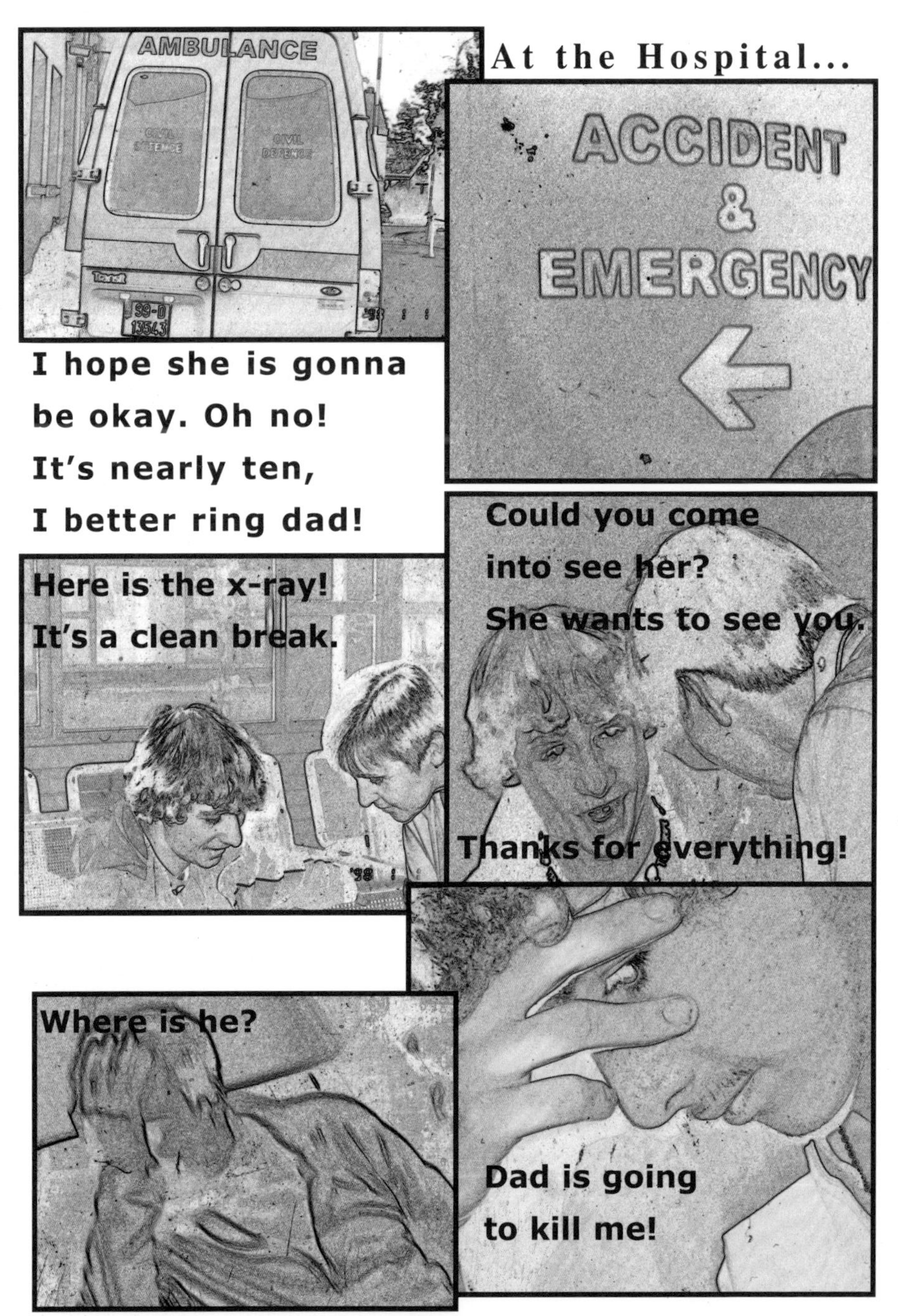

I hope he's okay, maybe I was too harsh.
I never knew it was this hard.

Dad I'm really sorry, let me explain.

GET TO YOUR ROOM!

Some Time Later...

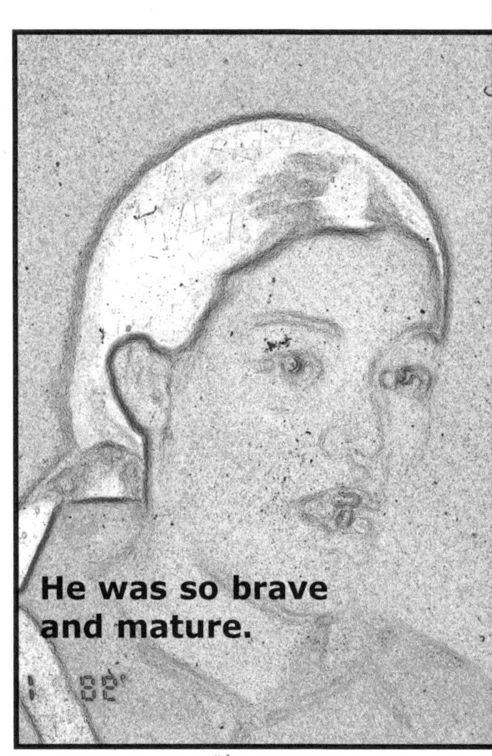

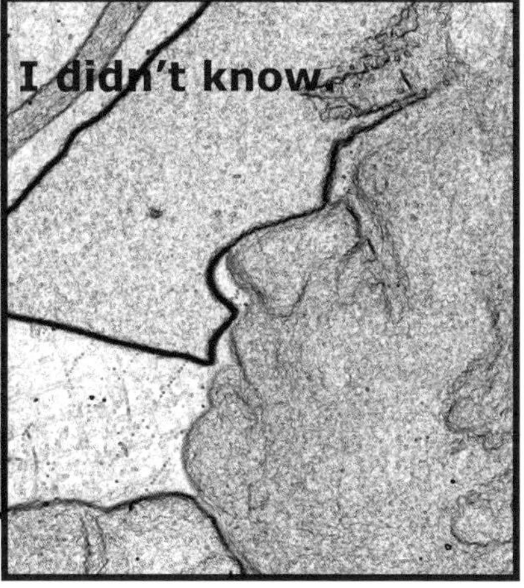

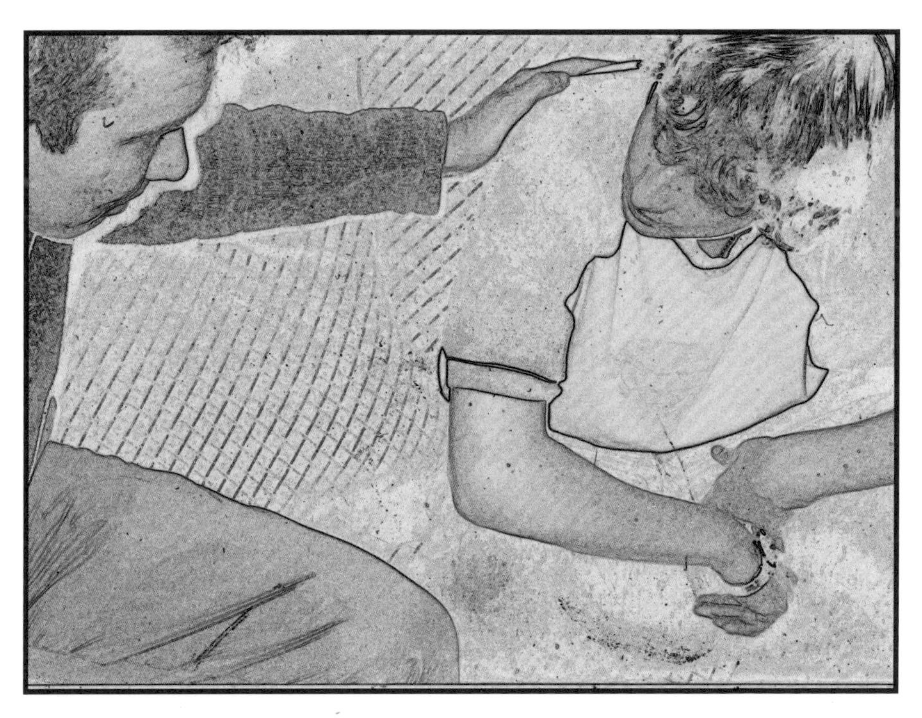

I'm sorry, I wasn't trusting you for the past year or so. From now on I want us to get along. I just don't know how to, a lot of the time.

Can we try again?

Hi Mum, things are getting better with Dad. He is starting to trust me now my curfew is back to normal. We discussed all the rules together and we get along together better now. Chloe's getting better now, she broke her leg and sprained her wrist. She'll be out of hospital soon. Still I wish you were here.

I miss you so much! I love you.

Why we wrote this story

We are a group of four young people (2 boys and 2 girls) aged 14 -16 years and 2 adult leaders. We wrote this story because we often feel that we are not treated as we would want. We want to have a say in our lives and our rules and sometimes adults can't understand this. We want to be listened to.

How we wrote this story

We sat down together and brainstormed the most common problems among us in our families. The most common problems were Fighting, Separation and Conflict over rules in different houses. We wanted to write a story about these issues. There were five stages to writing this story:

1. We wrote the story out roughly.
2. We acted out the story, improvising the scenes.
3. We took photos while acting.
4. We stuck the photos on a mock up of the book.
5. Using a scanner we transferred the information to computer and resized it.

We think it is a very interesting story and very relevant to teenagers and useful for adults!
We hope you do too.

What we want you to learn from this story...

If you are an adult.

We know parents hide a lot from their kids, but this leads to fighting and misunderstanding. We want to be honest and to be included in decisions that affect us. We are intelligent enough to understand what we need and can be responsible, if given a chance.

If you are a teenager:

You can understand that you are not alone and there are many others that feel the same as you. If you have recently lost a parent or a relative there a number of organisations who can help, these are listed below.

Rainbow Ireland:

Organises support groups nationally for children and young adults of bereaved or separated families.

Loreto Centre, Crumlin Road, Dublin 12. Tel: 01-473 4175

Solas - Bereavement Helpline: Advice and counselling line aimed at children and families following the death of a parent, carer or sibling.

Barnardos: Christchurch Square, Dublin 8.

Tel: 01-473 2110 (Mon-Fri 10.00am to 12.00pm)

ALMOST

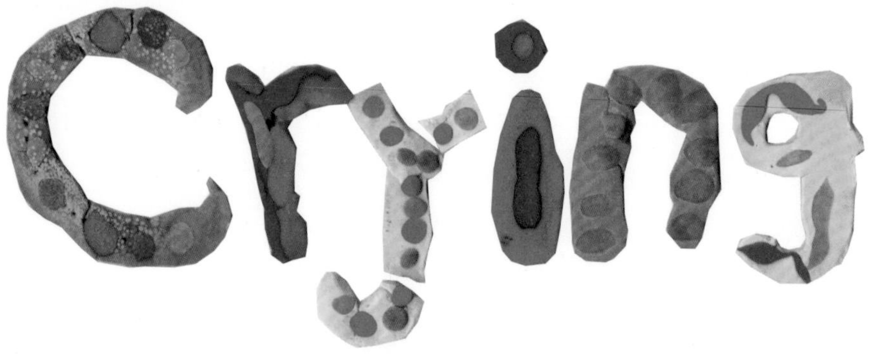
Crying

The Freaky Four are chatting in the park.

"I got a new CD."

"What CD did you get?"

"Did you hear my request on the radio?"

"I was up all night playing my computer game."

Blah, Blah, Blah, Blah!

Horms joins the group and asks Minnie,

"Did you make the basketball team?"

The Freaky Four ignore Horms and start playing football. When Horms joins them, they stop playing and head home. It is the same story at school, Horms is left out, and he wanders the school halls alone.

The Freaky Four are at their party.

Horm is left out again.

Minnie brings the Hi-Fi,

Handy brings the candy,

Heather takes her feather,

Iceman keeps cool.

Horms is outside looking in.

He feels left out, lonely and isolated.

Iceman comes to the door and sees

Horm looking in.

"Freeze!"

"What are you doing here?"

"You can't chill with us."

"You're causing a party meltdown."

Horm runs off. He is almost crying.

He runs home and dives under his bed.

Horm is in his safe place.

He is feeling unloved, terrible, sad, angry, lonely, depressed and suicidal.

"There is something missing from this party.

Guess who was outside?

He has been following us around for weeks now. He is always on his own, looking lost and lonely, looking in, wanting to be one of us,"

says Iceman.

The Freaky Four start to feel guilty.

Iceman begins to melt. He has a heart.

"You should have seen his face."

"He was almost crying."

The search is on.

They have already searched the park, football field, the riverside, the tall building and all the wardrobes.

The Freaky Four find Horm under his bed.

"Come join our party, I lost my cool."

The group walk back to the house together.
"What's the name of this gang," asks Horm.
"We are the Freaky Four," says Iceman
"Well how about renaming it,
The Fantastic Five," asks Horm.
"You're cool," says Iceman.

Minnie brought the hi-fi,

Handy found the candy,

Heather took her feather,

Iceman keeps cool,

Horm is the happiness.

Who we are?

We are 6 young people (3 boys and 3 girls) aged 12-15 years and 3 adult leaders from Athy, Co Kildare. We thought about friendships – we talked about what it would be like to have no friends.
We worked on the sets for each story – the group decided that the story would be cartoonish, alien and different. We moulded models from clay to form the characters in the story. We designed the sets and photographed the finished work.
When other people ignore us we feel:
Bullied, isolated, lonely, suicidal, unsafe, left-out, different, unaccepted, disrespected, angry, unwanted.

Who could use this story?

5th and 6th class children in primary schools and 1st and 2nd year secondary students. We feel that the story could be used as a role play to bring up the issue of bullying, why people do it, why some people are bullied and others are not, what they do when they are bullied, etc. The story could also be used to look at the importance of friendships in young people's lives.

Why we enjoyed this project.

Being part of this project meant we had a part to play, working together, building new friendships, working through the process, achieving the final result, travelling out of the local area, meeting new people and being part of a new environment, being listened to, learning to stick with things until they are finished. At the end of the story we had more confidence, felt a sense of ownership and achievement, were happy and relieved it all came together, developed a better understanding about what it felt like to be discriminated against, felt supported and treated fairly by adults who understood us and talked to us and not at us.

UP, UP

AND

DOWN

Stephen Wickham's father got a new job and had to move town to live in Dublin city. Stephen finds it hard to fit in with the other kids at his new school and is really depressed. He would do almost anything to make new friends.
These are extracts from Stephen's diary.

Today as usual, was a bad day! Paul McCartney knew what he was on about, "yesterday all my troubles seemed so far away." In my old school I had loads of friends, here I have none. Everyone has their own group and I can't get into them. I have nothing to do after school but watch T.V. I have to eat lunch alone. All the cool ones smoke so I think if I did, it might help; but I don't want to damage my health! But I am going to have to do something.

20th September

Finally, I have met a really cool gang, a few days ago! There's about five boys and three girls. One of the girls is really nice (and good looking). She's called Sammy and she is fifteen.
It's great to be accepted and feel part of a group, because the other day someone was shouting abuse at me and they all stood up for me. Paul even pinned him up against a wall! But they are always talking about "being stoned" and taking drugs. I've no clue what they are talking about, but I said that I took hash before, in case they laughed at me.

8th October

Bad night last night. It started well but got worse and worse. I went to a party at Paul's last night. Everyone was skinning up joints. I felt a little awkward and stupid becauwse they all knew what they were at. I bluffed my way through, when I smoked hash I tried my best not to cough but I couldn't help it. They didn't laugh at me! I got really stoned and got the giggles (and hungry). I chatted to Sammy. We got on well. I think she likes me too. After a while I got really sick and puked everywhere. I lay on the floor in the bathroom for the rest of the night.

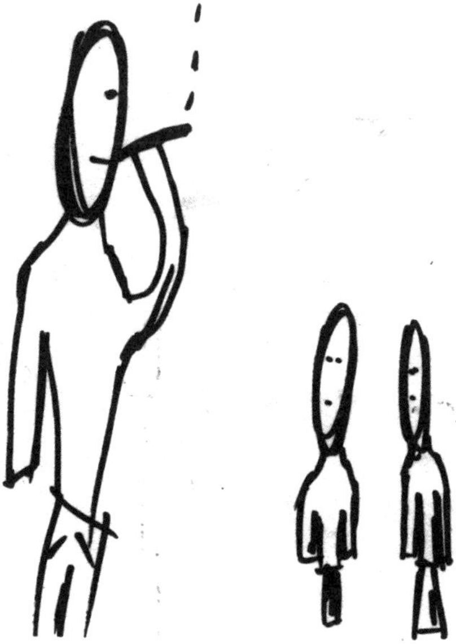

After taking hash that night, I said I'd never do it again. A few nights ago, the gang went out to a night club. I got pretty drunk but a few of the lads were taking E's. It looked easier than hash and they looked to be having a great buzz.
I bought white runners and a hoodie, that's what all the lads wear. They always listen to dance music, I prefer rock. If I tell them I like rock music they wouldn't like me, so I'll keep it to myself.
Next time we go out I think I'll try ecstasy!

17th November

Well boy! We went to the best club last night, it was banging tunes all night. I got a E-tab off Paul for €8. It's way easier to take than hash, just put it in your mouth and swallow. I didn't feel different at first, after a half an hour I was bananas. I felt warm and happy. I could talk to anyone. I had the courage to go out and dance, I was going mental. I was with Sammy. The ecstasy gave me the courage to ask her out, she said yes. I felt on top of the world.

3rd December

I got my report back from school, Dad and Mam went mental. I failed three subjects. Sure it's not like I need to be able to speak French and all that crap. I got the nickname 'T-rex 'off the lads, don't ask me why. Me and Sammy are going out with each other. I have heard things about her but I don't think they are true. One of the lads says he knows someone that has a party tonight, he's gonna try to nick his parents motor and collect us.
It's going to be a good night. I can't believe how good things are going. I really finally fit in.

17th December

School News School News School News

The staff and pupils at St. Fredrick's College would like to extend their condolences to the family and friends of Stephen Wickham who died so tragically on Friday last 17th of December.

In the short time we knew Stephen we realise what a great loss his death will be for all of us.

Due to the circumstances of Stephen's death, by drug overdose, the school will now be developing a drug awareness campaign. Together we can ensure this tragedy will never be repeated.

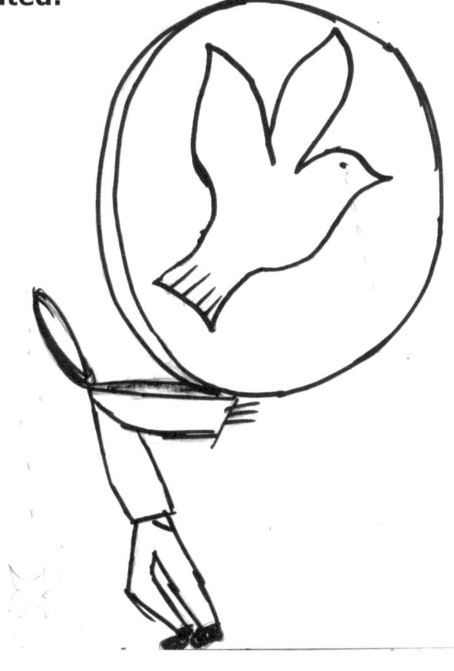

D r u g s K i l l

Ecstasy, chemical name MDMA, is a very common drug with ravers because of the happy, sociable, emotionally open feeling it causes in users. In 2002 over 39% of people over the age of 16 said they have used ecstasy and 52% of people over 16 know people who have taken it. It is a difficult drug to classify, being neither a true hallucinogen, like LSD, nor a true stimulant like amphetamine itself. Some researchers have coined the term 'entactogen' to describe its apparently unique effect including closeness to others, facilitating relationships and creating empathy. Ecstasy is sold mainly as tablets with a variety of logos imprinted on them. Over 200 logos have been observed in Europe, including many Disney characters, $ and £ signs. The main 'brands' appear to be those bearing the Mitsubishi triple diamond logo but other popular ones include 'shamrock' and in this case 'doves'. Deaths resulting from ecstasy use are relatively rare but since they involve young people they are particularly tragic. Deaths can be due to a variety of causes ranging from delusional behaviour to heart attacks, strokes and asthma attacks.

Drugs Kill

In Carrickmacross our group organises events and fundraising activities which are all Drug and Alcohol Free events and all the proceeds go to the local youth centre for facilities for young people. Remember, drugs kill people. Don't be foolish enough to think it won't kill you. Instead of taking that drug, come down to the youth centre and get involved in activities. Remember it's your life, don't drug it up.

This story is about Bullying and the issues associated with it. It shows us how young people can really cover their problems, not letting the rest of their friends or family know what is really happening in their lives. It is also written from our perspective which is great.

It all began at nine o'clock, with the hustle and bustle of school life. Emma and Clara collected their books and headed off to the first class of the day. 
"You look really tired, are you okay?" asked Emma.
"Yeah I'm grand. It's just my sister was sick last night and I had to look after her," sighed Clara.
Clara's mother died last year, leaving Clara to look after her little brothers and sisters.
"What class is next?" asked Emma,
"Maths, we've got a test." replied Clara.
"I completely forgot! Why give us a test after the weekend?" Emma groaned.
"It's easy, only co-ordinate geometry, we've been doing it for ages!" said Clara.
"Says you, you never get less than 90% and I usually look over your shoulder to scrape a pass!" retorted Emma.

They turned down the corridor and were faced with Angus.
The reactions on their faces were polar opposites of each other; Clara frowned while Emma beamed.
"Hey Angus!" said Emma.
Angus shoved Jack once more into the locker.
"Hi Emma, what's up?" he grinned.
Clara helped Jack up,
"Are you okay Jack?" she asked, concerned.
"Just about, I better go now quickly," he said.
Clara watched Jack scurry off. It was the only thing he was good at, running. She sighed and dragged Emma away from Angus and into their classroom.
Clara was right, the test was easy, but Emma still couldn't do it.

"Psst, Clara, how do you do number eight?"
Emma whispered. 
"Is that all you care about?"
Clara hissed back.
"What's wrong with you?"
Emma said, startled.
"You don't care at all about what sort of person you're going out with, do you?"
Clara burst out. "
"You don't care how terrible he is to other people, do you?"
"Well, you don't know about Angus,"
returned Emma,
"His Mum's horrible, she drinks the whole time and his Dad is hardly ever at home. He wants to help but he can't. He's so frustrated with his life!"
The bell rang and Emma stormed out. She dumped her books on a windowsill, still fuming over the row. She strode through the side-door, not noticing the other people crowding the corridors.

She encountered Angus.
"Angus, I need to talk to you," she said sharply.
"Why?" Angus asked. 
"Just because, okay?"
she retorted.
"Why do you always pick on
Jack, what did he ever do to
you?" she asked him.
"He's just Jack. I don't need
a reason!" he laughed.
"You know how messed up he
is? It's your fault, he wouldn't be
so bad if it wasn't for you!" she shouted at him.
"What do you mean, what's wrong with him?"
Angus asked, puzzled.
"Do you not know how depressed he is?"
Clara says he is so nervous and afraid of what
other people think of him," explained Emma,
"he's been going to a psychiatrist for the last
year now. His life is so messed up and you're not
helping the situation. He wishes to be more con-
fident, like you."
"Still that's his problem.
I don't want to be like him anyway." says Angus.
"That's not fair, you don't even know him."

"And I don't want to!"

"Fine, if that's your attitude!"

Emma turned and walked off. Clara went around lonely for the next few days. Emma was avoiding her. Whenever they met in the corridor Emma would just pass without a glance. Clara noticed she was looking paler and sick. Also she noticed Jack wasn't in school at all. She guessed he was avoiding Angus. Angus himself was going around with a scowl permanently fixed on his face.

Clara confronts Angus, she wants to know what's going on between him and Emma.

"Have you been talking to Emma lately?"

"No, not since Monday"

"But that was four days ago!
What happened?"

"I don't know she just got all sentimental over Jack."

"OVER JACK?! I didn't think she cared about him."

"Well she might but I don't,
no matter what she says!"
"You are such an idiot Angus!"
"It's not my fault she's got an attitude problem."
"Look at you, you're not such a perfect person yourself!" "Get out of my face now!"
Clara walks off in a huff.

Next Monday, during lunch, Angus goes looking for Emma but she is nowhere to be found. Angus spots Clara over the lunchroom and decides to try to end the row. He calls her over.
"Hey Clara!"
"What do you want?"
"I was just wondering, if you know where Emma is?"
"I was just about to ask you the same question. She is in, I saw her on the bus this morning."
Clara and Angus go looking for Emma. Twenty minutes later after searching everywhere with no luck, Clara decides to try the bathrooms. She goes in and hears what sounds like somebody being sick. She searches the bathrooms and just as she is about to leave Emma emerges from the bathroom looking paler than she has been all week.
"Are you okay?"

"Yes, I'm grand."
"Was that you getting sick?"
Suddenly Emma bursts into tears,
"Oh Clara, help me please?"
What is it?" Is it Angus?"
"It's everything, it's been going on
for ages, everyday."
"Is it your family, is there something
wrong?"
Are you pregnant?" Emma freezes.
Clara walks out saying, "Oh my God,
I can't believe it," over and over to
herself. After what seems likes hours, Clara
encounters Angus in the corridor.
"Do you have any idea what you've done to her?"
"None what so ever! What did I do?"
"She's pregnant for God sake!"
"What? It was our first time. I don't
believe this, how? what? when?!"
"She just told me now"
"The cheating little..."
"Don't dare talk about her like that
since it's probably all your fault
anyways."
Angus storms off looking for Emma
to set the record straight.
He finds Emma in tears.

"Why didn't you tell me sooner?"

"So Clara told you then?"

"Yeah, he sighs, how long have you been like this?"

"Little over a year."

"That's not possible, so you're not pregnant then?"

"PREGNANT! No, I'm bulimic, where did you get that idea, you eejit?"

"But Clara said..."

Clara comes around the corner.

"Clara, I'm bulimic you idiot, not pregnant!"

"You're bulimic????? Oh My God!"

"But how could we have missed that? We see each other everyday and we've missed everything that's been going on in our lives. Emma, you say that this has been going on for little over a year, A YEAR! Looking at it now, it seems so obvious, how could you have lost all that weight in so little time? "Angus, look at you! All this time we've known each other, I didn't know that your mother is an alcoholic and your father he's never at home, all this time, I just thought you were an arrogant pig.

I’m so sorry. And Jack, look at Jack! Up until a few days ago none of us knew he was depressed, how could we miss that?”
Clara stops talking.
“Clara, what about you?”
“What do you mean, Emma?”
“Clara, your mother died last year, you instantly took over her role, you never got time to grieve, you constantly mind you brothers and sisters and your father is never there, that’s not what a 15 year old’s life should be like”
Angus interrupts Emma.
“Clara, your mother died ? I’m sorry, I didn’t know. I think you’re right, we’ve known each other all this time and don’t really know each other. Where is Jack? Let’s go find him. I want to say I’m sorry to him, I never understood him. I was too wrapped up in my own life to know what’s going on in his life. We all were.” The friends walk off together to find Jack,
all knowing each other, Inside Out.

Who wrote this story?

The Midlands Regional Youth Service publishing group consists of:
Erinna Foley-Fisher, Paul Kilroy-Glynn,
Lorraine Nally, Aisling O' Brien, all from Athlone and its environs, co-ordinated by Eileen Kelly, Development Officer with the organistion.
We are in transition year in secondary school. We got involved in this project because of an interest in media studies and a need to do something new and different. This helped with school studies and offered a wonderful opportunity to be creative. One of the members of our group is interested in journalism and hopes to pursue a career in this area.

We envisage the story could be used as an introductory programme in a session dealing with bullying in a youth work or school setting. It could also be used as a drama sketch to introduce the issues, where the young people could be given different roles and act out the characters using the dialogue in the book.

Text could be modified or changed if necessary. This story could also be used to introduce a teenage pregnancy programme or sexual health programme with a group of teenagers. What if Emma was pregnant instead of bulimic?

The End

Kids' Own Publishing Partnership
Kingsfort Studios
Ballintogher
Co. Sligo
Republic of Ireland
Tel: +353 (0) 71 916 4438
Fax: +353 (0) 71 916 4458
info@kidsown.ie
www.kidsown.ie

National Youth Federation,
20 Lower Dominick Street,
Dublin 1
Tel: +353 (0) 1 872 9933
Fax:+353 (0) 1 872 4183
info@nyf.ie
www.nyf.ie

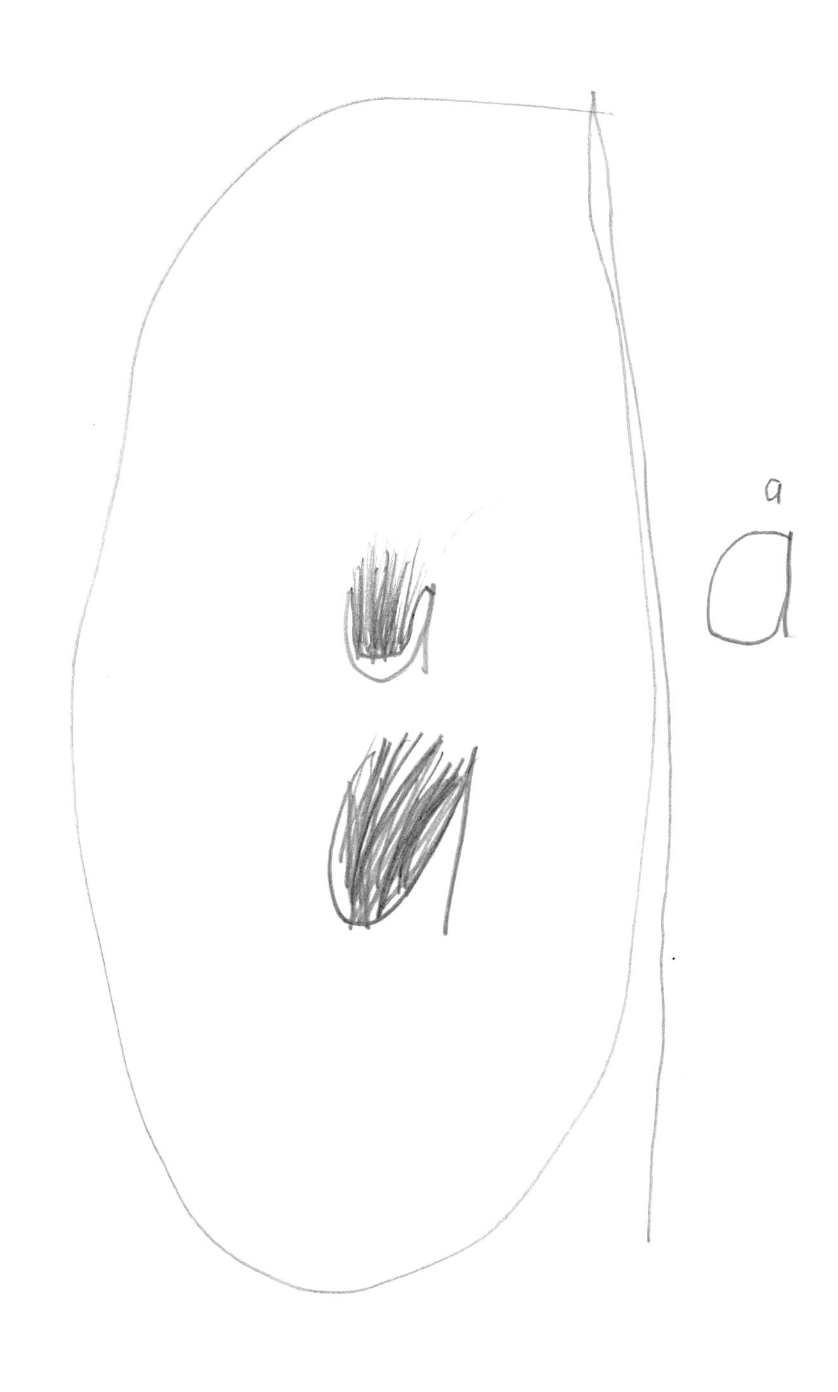